Taking My Cat to the Vet

by Susan Kuklin

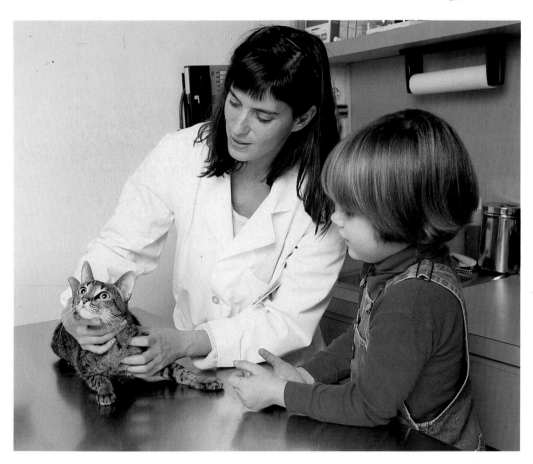

Bradbury Press New York

With special thanks to:

Ben Homrighausen

Lindsley and David Homrighausen

Sarah Homrighausen

Dr. Dale Rubin

The staff at the Gramercy Park
    Animal Hospital

Sharon Steinhoff

Dr. Jay D. Kuhlman

Julie Quan

Karrie Perkins

Bradbury Press
An Affiliate of Macmillan, Inc.
866 Third Avenue, New York, N.Y. 10022
Collier Macmillan Canada, Inc.
Printed and bound in the United States of America

10 9 8 7 6 5 4 3 2 1

LIBRARY OF CONGRESS CATALOGING-IN-PUBLICATION DATA
Kuklin, Susan.
Taking my cat to the vet.

Summary: Ben takes his cat Willa to the veterinarian,
watches the medical examination, and hears about various
health problems his cat might encounter in the future.
1. Cats—Diseases—Juvenile literature.
2. Veterinary hospitals—Juvenile literature. [1. Cats—
Diseases. 2. Veterinary hospitals. 3. Veterinary
medicine.] I. Title.
SF985.K85 1988   636.8′0896   88-5052
ISBN 0-02-751233-9

Willa was a kitten when we got her from the A.S.P.C.A. adoption truck. Right away, Mom and Dad took her to the doctor who takes care of animals, a veterinarian, for shots and a checkup.

Now that Willa is one year old, the vet wants to look her over at least once a year. My older sister Sarah usually goes with Mommy to the vet. But today it's my turn. How do you get a cat into her travel box?

Willa comes down from the ledge, then stops.

You can't tell a cat what to do!

Finally Sarah takes over. "Watch me, Ben," she says. Sarah wraps one arm around Willa's chest and the other arm around her rump. I lift the lid while she lowers Willa into the carrier.

The carrier has lots of holes so Willa has enough air. To make it soft and cozy, we put a large towel inside, plus her favorite toy. There's no food, water, or litter in the box because that would make a mess.

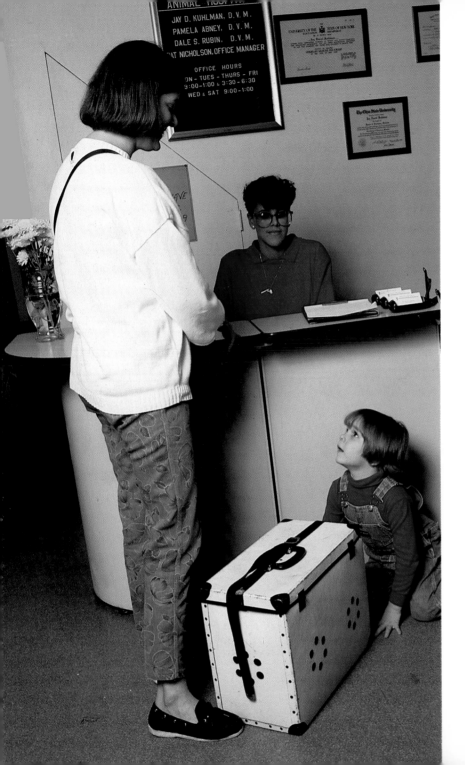

When we're finally at the vet's office,
I can't wait to sit down. Willa's carrier is
heavy!

"Can I take Willa out now?" I ask.

"No, not yet," Mommy answers.

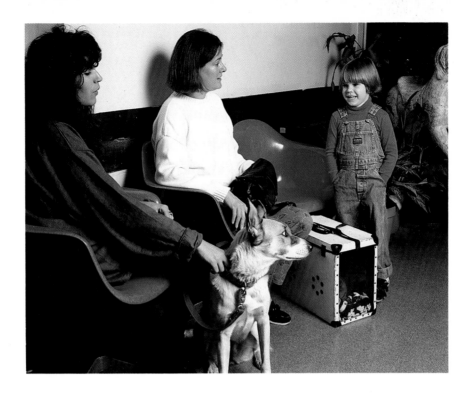

There are other people in the waiting room with their pets. I would love to pat the dog near me, but I don't. At home, Mommy explained that some of the animals here might be sick or might snap. So I just talk to the owner about her dog.

Willa has never seen a dog. Since this is a strange place, she's hiding in her box. That's good. If Willa ran loose, this big dog might really scare her!

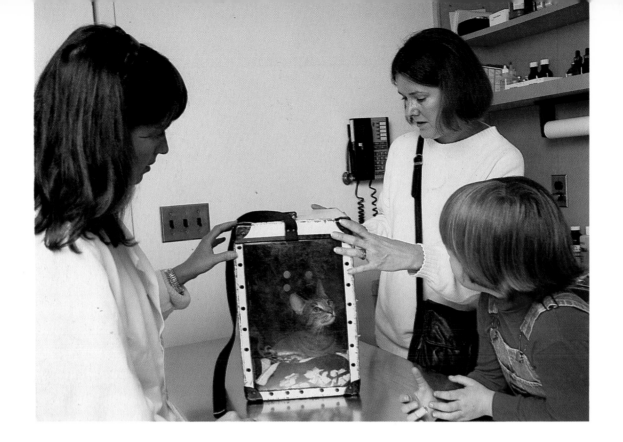

When our names are called, we carry Willa in her carrier to a small room with a long shiny table.

Dr. Rubin follows us in. "Hi," she says.

"I'm Ben," I tell her. "Mommy said I could come today."

The vet asks us lots of questions and writes some things on a card with Willa's name on it. Is Willa sick? Is she eating regularly? The doctor wants to know if we are having any special problems with Willa.

 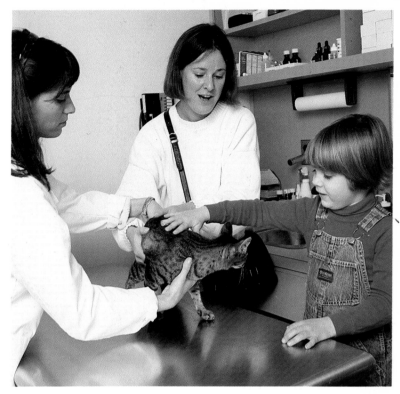

I tell her that Willa is great.

Dr. Rubin nods. "Okay, let's take Willa out now."

"There, there, little girl." Mommy talks to Willa to keep her calm.

"Now pat her," she says to me, as we lift Willa out of the box.

"Willa, Willa," I whisper.

"Willa doesn't bite or swipe, right?" Dr. Rubin asks.

"Right," I say. "Willa is a gentle cat."

"That makes my job easier." The doctor smiles. "Let's get started."

First, Dr. Rubin looks at Willa all over. "She seems to be in good shape," she tells us. "Willa has a shiny coat, bright eyes, and no runny nose. All those things are signs of a healthy cat."

Next, Dr. Rubin feels all over Willa's body. She starts at her neck. Then she checks her paws, nails, and feet. Last of all, the doctor gently presses all around my cat's belly. "I don't feel any bad bumps inside or outside Willa that could be a sign of disease," she says at last. "And Willa's insides are the right size and right where they should be."

"Now I need to examine Willa's eyes," Dr. Rubin says. "They are clear, just as they should be. If they were watery or teary, Willa might have a cold."

The vet pulls down Willa's eyelids to show me the bright pink skin around each eye. "The color is perfect," she tells me. "No signs of disease here.

"Now, if your mom can hold Willa again, I'll use the ophthalmoscope." The doctor explains that this tool lets her see deep inside Willa's eyes. Sometimes she knows a cat is sick by the way her eyes look. Not Willa—her eyes are fine.

Next, the doctor peers inside our cat's ears. "I don't see any scabs or crusts that could mean an infection," she says. "But I'll take a closer look with the otoscope."

Mommy holds Willa, and I ask, "What are you looking for?"

"Ear mites," the veterinarian says. "Very tiny insects that can make a cat's ears itch. Willa's ears are fine, though. Do you want to see?"

"What's that brown stuff?" I ask.

Dr. Rubin looks. "Wax, and it should come out." She takes a long Q-tip and gently cleans Willa's ears.

I watch while the vet opens Willa's mouth. "I'm checking her breath, her teeth, and her gums," she tells me. "Willa has sweet breath, clean teeth, and smooth pink gums. Perfect."

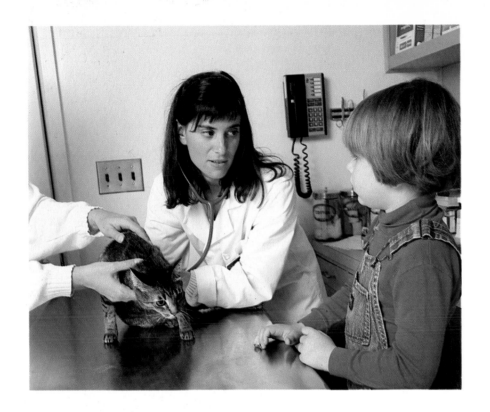

After Dr. Rubin has checked Willa's heart, she lets me listen with the stethoscope. "Willa's getting nervous," she tells me. "Her heart is beating pretty fast. But it's a nice regular beat."

At first I can't hear anything. Then the sound comes *thump, thump, thump.*

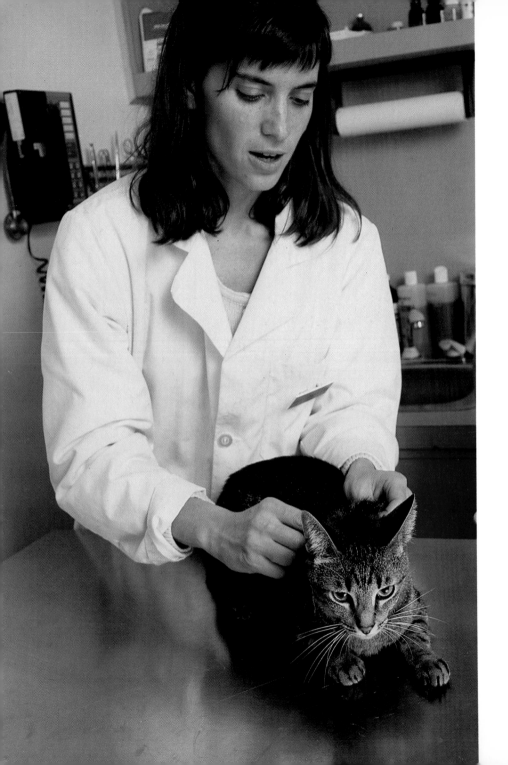

"You're such a good girl, Willa," Dr. Rubin whispers as she feels all over my cat again. This time, she tells me, she's looking for pimples or other skin lumps. Some are bad, others are okay. "If I saw any that might be a problem," she goes on, "I'd take them off and study them under the microsope."

Once again, Willa is fine.

"Willa's getting tired," Dr. Rubin says, "so help keep her calm while I trim her nails."

Because Willa is always inside, her nails don't need to be long and sharp. Usually my dad clips Willa's nails.

When Dr. Rubin moves her fingers through Willa's fur to check for fleas and ticks, Willa purrs. She likes this part.

"Could I get fleas?" I ask.

"No," Dr. Rubin explains. "Fleas hide in animal fur. But you could get ticks, which are slightly larger than fleas. If Willa had fleas or ticks, I would bathe her with special medicine."

I am glad to hear that Willa has no ticks or fleas.

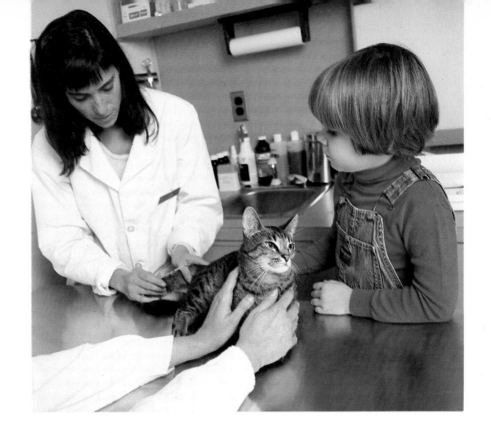

"Before I give Willa her shots," Dr. Rubin says, "I need to take her temperature." She asks for Mom's help. The thermometer has to stay in Willa's bottom for two minutes.

"Willa's temperature is normal," Dr. Rubin tells us. "It's 102 degrees. Anything between 101 and 102.8 degrees is fine."

Now Dr. Rubin asks me, "Have you ever had any shots called vaccinations, Ben?"

When I say yes, she explains that Willa's vaccinations are a little like mine because they protect her from some bad sicknesses. Today Willa is getting a shot for a disease called rabies and another to keep her safe from many different diseases. "Usually," Dr. Rubin adds, "she'd get a vaccination now for leukemia, too. But cats only get leukemia from other cats. And because Willa is just around people, she doesn't need that one.

"Willa may jump a bit, but these hardly hurt," the doctor tells me.

"There, good girl," Mommy and Dr. Rubin say, as the doctor gives Willa one shot in the back leg and one in the neck.

When the shots are over, I tell Willa she's a brave cat. She rubs against me to let me know she loves me, too.

The doctor puts Willa on a scale. She weighs 6¼ pounds. "That's an excellent weight for her size," Dr. Rubin tells us. "To keep her slim, feed her one small can of cat food two times a day. Also give her a little dry food to crunch on for her teeth. And keep a bowl of fresh water nearby.

"Try not to give Willa cat junk food or table food—especially chicken bones. They will make her choke."

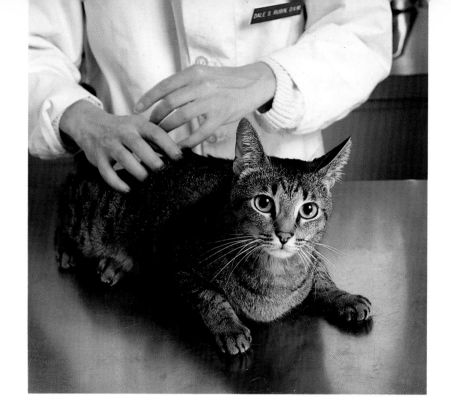

"Dr. Rubin, sometimes Willa throws up these yucky balls," I say.

"Usually, that's nothing to worry about," she explains. "Cats clean themselves every day by licking their coats. They swallow the loose fur that gets caught up in their sandpapery tongues. In their stomachs, this hair forms into balls. Cats will throw up these hair balls. If you brush Willa several times a week, she will have fewer hair balls."

When Dr. Rubin asks if we have any more questions, I know we're at the end. We can't think of anything else to ask.

"You have a fine, healthy cat," Dr. Rubin tells me. "Help me put her back in the carrier now."

Dr. Rubin writes on the record card while we get ready to go.

"Thank you, Doctor," Mommy says.

"Thank you, Dr. Rubin," I say. "When I grow up, I want to be a veterinarian."

KEYS FOR A SUCCESSFUL VISIT TO THE VET

AT HOME:

Bring a stool sample.

Place the cat in a secure carrier that is lined with a clean towel or blanket.

Put a small toy in the box, but leave out water, food, and litter.

Talk softly to your cat.

IN THE WAITING ROOM:

Keep the cat in her carrier.

Entertain yourself quietly.

Avoid touching the other animals.

Talk softly to your cat.

IN THE EXAM ROOM:

Keep your cat in the carrier until the veterinarian says to take her out.

Warn the veterinarian if your cat is nervous or tends to bite or swipe.

Listen carefully to the vet and talk only when it's your turn.

Stay calm to keep your cat calm.

During the exam, do not interrupt the vet or handle your pet unless asked to.

Be sure to keep hands off all tools and supplies.

AT HOME:

Give your cat a little water but do not feed right away.

Let your pet look around and feel secure.

Don't worry if your cat wants to be left alone. Otherwise, play gently and cuddle her.